-Crisis Z-

Made By

Leia F.L

-The chapters-

-Chapter 1-

-The drill-

I slept through the whole night for once. Without any nightmares. I slowly woke up to the smell of fresh rain. My window was slightly open. I looked at the clock, and there were still 12 minutes left, before my alarm would go off. So I laid down on my stomach, while enjoying the sound of the rain hitting the roof, and the cold air playing on my back. After 12 minutes, I sat up, and I looked out of the window. There was thunder outside. I texted Owen.

Owen♥

-You up?

Yeah, why?-

-Something just feels wrong.

Dw about it! You can always call me.-

-Thanks, I love you.

I Love you too.-

It made me feel a little bit better. I pushed the blanket aside, and put my feet down on my old rug. I decided to go wake up Dylan. I slowly opened his door, but to my surprise, he was already awake. He never wakes up by himself. "Hey, are you okay?" I asked him. "You know I hate thunder" he said. I sat down on his bed. "Well, as long as I'm here, I won't let anything hurt you. I promise" I said. He looked at me with a little smile, but he stayed silent. "I'm gonna go make you some breakfast, okay?" I said. He nodded and smiled. I went downstairs, and made a peanut butter and jelly sandwich, his favorite. I went upstairs, and gave it to him.

A figure appeared in the doorway. It was dad. I walked towards him with a little smile. "You do know you're a good big sister, right?" he whispered. My smile became bigger. He stroked my short, dark hair. "You know, when I look at you, I see mom" he said. "She would be so proud of you" he continued. "That's the best compliment ever" I said. He smiled. I went to my room, and packed my stuff for school. "Come on

Dylan, we don't wanna miss the bus!" I shouted. He came downstairs, and we ran outside to the bus. I saw Owen in the back, so I went down there, and hugged him tight. There were still a lot of thunder and lightning, but I enjoyed it. Me and my mom would always look at it from her window, so it reminds me of her. "Hey, are you okay?" Owen asked me. Then I realized I had zoned out. "I'm fine" I answered.

I noticed that Caleb entered the bus. He came down to us, and I smiled. Caleb is my best friend too. Me, him and Owen, have been best friends since we were 4. Caleb is more like a brother to me than a friend. He was in Canada when my mom went missing, that's why I'm closer to Owen now.

Before I knew it, we were at the school. As I walked out of the bus, I felt something. It was the same feeling I got earlier. Something just felt wrong. I couldn't tell what it was. I looked up at the sky. A big group of birds were flying towards the opposite direction of the school. I felt someone's touch on my hand. Warm fingers held mine. It was Owen. "Are you okay?" he asked. I nodded. He squeezed my hand, before slowly letting go of it. It was starting to get really windy. I felt the hairs sticking out of my ponytail, tickling on my face, as the wind was controlling their movements. I heard the bell ring, so I ran inside to my first class. We just had some time to do our unfinished homework. After some time, we had a break. The thunder was getting really bad.

Everything went by so fast, and before I knew it, it was lunch time. I sat with Owen and Caleb as usual. I felt a little bit dizzy, but it wasn't that bad. As I sat there and ate my food, Owen and Caleb played rock, paper, scissor shoot. They always finish eating so fast, I can't keep up anymore. "You're taking ages" Caleb said, laughing quietly. I gave him my death stare, and then took the last bite of my burger. "See you after school dorks" I said while walking away. As I walked down the hallway, I noticed some girls giving me weird looks. They always do that. I rolled my eyes and kept walking. I went into the bathroom. I had to make sure, that I didn't have any food in my teeth. As I was looking in the mirror, I noticed how pale I was. I shook it off and left the bathroom.

The day flew by, and I was sitting in my last class. I was in the middle of a test. There was silence, until a siren went off. We do a lot of drills here, one every week, so I know *every* single siren, but I didn't recognize this one. I sat so still, trying to figure out which one it was. Then I slowly found it familiar. I had heard about it on Youtube. It was a zombie siren. *No, we're NOT in a zombie apocalypse.* It was just weird, I mean the teachers always tell us, when a drill is going to go off, so we're prepared and aware. I looked at my teacher, and she was frozen, but she was slightly shaking too, and that was the moment I realized, that it wasn't a drill.

-END OF 1ST CHAPTER-

-Chapter 2-

-The escape-

I started to sweat. *Was this really happening? What about Dylan, Owen, Caleb and dad!?* I was out of my body. Some people turned to me, because they know, that I know what siren this is. "It's a Zombie siren" I mumbled. Everyone looked up at the teacher, who was still frozen. She nodded. "Yeah...Yeah she's right" she said, staring at the floor. "Oh my god" someone said. Everyone started freaking out, and some started crying. "But, but it's...it's just a drill, right?!" Aimee asked while panicking. There was silence. Everyone prayed that the teacher would say it was. "No...No it's not..." I answered, while looking down at my desk. I felt everyone staring at me. The speakers went on: "Everyone, GET ON THE FOOTBALL FIELD....this is not a drill!"

I ran, I ran faster than ever. I didn't care about the others in my class, I only cared about my family and friends. Almost the whole school were at the football field. It was extremely crowded.

"OWEN!? CALEB!? DYLAN!?" I yelled from
the top of my lungs. I couldn't see them
anywhere, there were too many people. I kept on
looking. I was out of breath, but I still managed
to shout: "OWEN". I was almost crying. Then I
saw them, I saw Owen and Caleb. When I made
eye contact with them, we all ran to each other. I
hugged them tight. "Dylan, where's Dylan?!
Have you seen Dylan?" I asked them, while
panicking. "I...I don't know" Owen replied.
"DYLAN!" I kept on shouting. That was the
moment my heart skipped a beat. He wasn't on
the field, he was on the other side of the fence,
on the road. My breathing was shaky. "Dylan?"
I whispered in shock. I ran as fast as I could. I
pushed people to get through, because it was so
crowded. "DYLAN!" I yelled. We made eye
contact. "What are you doing out there!?" I
shouted at him. "I was on the toilet, but when I
came back, everyone in my class were gone" he
said. "Get in here, NOW!".
"What, why?" he asked.
"Because if you don't, you're gonna get killed, so
now GET IN!" I said quickly. He tried to climb,

but the fence was high. A tall figure appeared in the corner of my vision. My heart completely stopped. There it was, the very first zombie I had ever seen. But it was coming towards us...Towards Dylan. "Dylan...DYLAN HURRY UP!" I screamed. He looked back and saw it. He froze, he froze in the moment he wasn't supposed to. "NOW!" I screamed loudly, so loud, that everyone heard. That's when everyone saw it too. The ugly, brainless zombie, that was trying to kill my brother...All of us. Dylan got to the top of the fence, *right* when the zombie came too. He jumped down. I hugged him while he was crying. "Oh my god..." I said in relieve. I think he injured his foot when he landed, it was a really high fence. I quickly grabbed his wrist and stepped back from the zombie. There it was, right on the other side of the fence...And it brought its friends. All of a sudden, a whole group of zombies, were right in front of us. I called dad, he was on his way to pick me, Dylan, Caleb and Owen up. When his car parked, it took all of the zombies attention. "DAD!" I screamed. He started the car again, while all the zombies were coming towards him. He drove as fast as he could, I barely blinked, and there were dead zombies laying all over the ground.

"GET IN KIDS!" he shouted. Dylan couldn't walk, because of his foot, so I had to carry him. I felt everyone staring. When we were all on the other side and got in the car, my dad drove as fast as he could. We had to get to a safe place. Like a bunker or something. My dad knew everything about that, so we just trusted him. I didn't care about the others at the school, only the people in the car. I looked out of the window. I saw a zombie attacking a young woman. Owen saw it too. He took my hand, but this time, he didn't let go. *I can't believe this, we're actually in a zombie apocalypse. This is ACTUALLY happening.* We drove for hours. There were people in pain everywhere, because the zombies attacked them. How could it spread *so* fast? Some people just aren't quick enough. It was night when we finally arrived at the bunker, that we were going to stay in. We took everything from the car, in the bunker, but it was in a rush. The bunker smelled really bad. The smell was like a combination of underwear, and too old cheese. It was a big bunker. "So this is it? We're just gonna live here forever?" Dylan said aggressively. "For a while, yes...But there is something that can stop them, the zombies. We just have to figure out what it is, or wait until someone else does" my dad said calmly. Dylan was frustrated, I could tell. "I'm going to sleep" he said. I rubbed his back before he walked away. "This is so unfair" I said while staring at the wall. "I know" my dad replied. "Do you think our parents are alive?" Caleb asked. My dad took a deep breath. "I hope they are" he said. After an hour, everyone were going to bed. I grabbed Owen's wrist. "Look uh...I'm really sorry that we didn't get your parents. All I could think about was just your, Dylan's, Caleb's and my dad's safety. I didn't think about your family and I'm sorry" I said. He stayed silent. "Maybe we can go find them sometime" I said. "Maybe" he replied, before he went to his bed. I felt horrible, but I had to walk it off. I stared at Owen's back for a long time, before closing my eyes and going to sleep.   **-END OF 2ND CHAPTER-**

-CHAPTER 3-
-THE MISSION-

The next couple of days was just us planning to get Owen's and Caleb's parents, and finding a bigger bunker, that wasn't already taking by other survivors. I really hope we're going to find them. They would be broken if we don't. Owen didn't really talk to me that much. He didn't really talk that much in general. I think he's mad at me, and I don't blame him. We were going to drive to our neighborhood, and search for his and Caleb's parents. It was a couple of minutes before we were gonna look for them. I really needed to talk to Owen. "Owen, you got a minute?" I asked him. He nodded and we walked over to the corner. "I'm really, really sorry. But we will find them, I know we will!". "I'm not mad at you, okay?" he said. "What?". "It's just, I was there when you lost your mom and....I remember how much you were going through, and I'm just scared I'm gonna end up like that too" he said. I smiled awkwardly and hugged him. I was about to say something, but my dad interrupted me. "Ready to go?" he said. I took a deep breath and followed him to the car. We were driving for a couple of hours, until we finally got there.

The neighborhood looked...terrible. There was blood, and a couple of people in pain while transforming into zombies. It looked so abandoned. Dylan stayed in the car, while me and the others were going around, looking for Owen's and Caleb's parents. We split up, so me and Owen went in his house. We were quiet and had our guns ready. We checked every single room...nothing. "I'm so sorry..." I said to Owen. There was silence, but not for too long. I heard someone whimpering. Owen heard it too. It came from the bedroom. We walked in there. It was coming from the closet. I had my gun ready, while slowly opening the closet door. There she was, Owen's mom. She was crying, but she looked so relieved when she saw that it was just us, and not zombies. She ran to Owen and hugged him. "Dad...Where's dad?" he asked. His mom were looking at him while tearing up, but she was staying silent. "No..." Owen whispered to himself. His mom couldn't get a word out. He was dead. Owen's dad was dead.....Or turning into a monster...A zombie. After some time I heard something, and I knew exactly what it was. "Shoot! I really think we gotta go!" I said. I sounded like a dork, but if we didn't run now, we were gonna regret it. I took Owen's hand while running outside. His mom was right behind us. A zombie was standing in the door opening. It looked familiar, I think it's our neighbor, Victor. I knew Owen and his mom were scared, but I didn't hesitate. I shot it. They both stood there in shock. *Oh my god. I just killed someone.* I felt like a monster for killing Victor...But in the end, he was already dead...He wasn't himself anymore. I felt like throwing up. We finally made it out to the car, with zombies right behind us. Caleb's parents were there too. I hugged my dad. "Where's Mark?" he asked. Owen's mom stayed silent, while looking down. Mark was my dad's best friend, so he was hurt. A tear dropped down from his eye. He started driving to the new bunker. It was far away. Like days away. Most of the days were silent. Nothing happened.

Sometimes I'd notice, that Owen was silently crying, but I didn't want to comfort him, but give him space instead. I know that that's what he prefers. Not talking to Owen felt more lonely than being alone. I just sat in the corner, staring out of the window, watching people transforming. There was no hope, it felt empty. Everything did. After 3 horrible days, we arrived at the new bunker. There were more zombies now than ever. I can't imagine loosing more people. I mean, if it's going to feel like the time I lost mom, then I'm not gonna be able to do it...Not again.
We went in the bunker, and packed out everything. I didn't realize I had zoned out, until I felt Owen's hand on my shoulder. I turned around to see him slightly smiling. I was a bit shocked that he took contact to me. I didn't have the energy to fake a smile back, so I just looked away. He pulled me into a hug. Being in his arms felt amazing. I've really been needing it, and I bet he has too. I slowly pulled away. I looked him right in the eyes, with a numb feeling. I turned around, and walked away to help dad

with the table. "Need help?" I asked him. "I got it!". "Alright".

I didn't really know what to do. I walked to my bed and sat down. I was staring at the wall. I felt so hopeless, that it's unimaginable. I didn't even notice Caleb was staring at me. "You good?" he asked with a quiet voice. "I wish I had the energy to fake a yes" I said while still staring at the wall. I could hear him step closer and closer. He rubbed his hand on my back. "Everything is going to be fine" he said. "Bullshit" I said while laughing. "Can you maybe try to focus on the positives?". "There's absolutely nothing positive about this" I said. "Here we go again!". "And what is that supposed to mean?" I asked while turning around, and facing him. "You're always being so negative!". "So you're telling me, that you don't care about this whole zombie thing!?". "That's not what I said!". "Sure it wasn't". "It sucks! I know it does! But it's not getting better with no motivation" he said. "It's not like we can be saved". "We don't know that if we don't try!". "Could you stop pretending we're in a movie or something? You're being a little dramatic" I said while turning around again. "Now I get why Owen can't deal with you!" he said while walking away. "What is that supposed to mean?" I asked with pure confusion. "You know exactly what it means" he said before walking off. I felt a bit betrayed. I thought Owen was always honest with me...What has he been going around and saying behind my back?

-END OF 3RD CHAPTER-

-CHAPTER 4-
-THE SECRET-

I couldn't sleep that night. I kept thinking about what Caleb said. *What did he mean?* I acted like it didn't make sense, even though it kind of did. But there was still a lot I didn't know about it. I was so tired, but all the unknown secrets kept me awake. My eyes had bags under them, my hair looked gross, and I couldn't stop overthinking everything. I knew I wasn't going to sleep, so I sat up, and walked to the kitchen. I turned on the radio, it said weird noises for a while, until it broke through.

A zombie apocalypse has hit us, very badly. Right now, it's looking really bad in Novaly. Stay in a safe place, and don't let anyone in. We really-

The radio went out. Novaly...that's where I'm from. I guess I've been really lucky, getting out of there. Everything felt terrible. I was shaking. "Dana?". I turned around. Owen was standing behind me. "Can I talk to you, for a second?" I asked. "Sure". "Okay uhm...So me and Caleb had a fight, and...he said: "Now I get why Owen can't deal with you". And I figured, you would know what he's talking about..." I explained. He took a long breath and looked down. He only does that if he's ashamed, so it's not exactly a good sign. "Look uhm...Since me and Sophie became friends again, you've just been acting kind of jealous and distant..." he said while avoiding my eyes. "Okay, I have been jealous. But what do you want me to do? She's your ex, of course I'm skeptical. And I mean...everyone thinks that you're back together" I said. He was now facing me. "Remember why we broke up in the first place? I left her to be with you! How can you be jealous?" he said. "Well It's not my fault that I have normal, human being feelings, like every other person!" I said in frustration. He raised his voice. "Just learn how to control it! You've only got me and Caleb, so you should be more careful. We can disappear as fast as we appeared, and then you've got no one left. What will you do then, huh?".

After quickly realizing what he had just done, I could see the regret in his eyes. "I- I'm sorry. I didn't mean it". I was hurt. A lot. I would rather transform into a zombie right now, than to be in this situation. I raised my eyebrows in anger and scoffed. I walked past him, but he grabbed my wrist. "Don't touch me!" I said, pulling my wrist to myself. He was about to say something, probably apologize, but I walked away before he had the chance. I went back to bed in anger. Now I definitely couldn't sleep. That's what he's been keeping from me. That's his little secret. I obviously couldn't sleep, but I needed to save strength, so I closed my eyes and relaxed for another 3-4 hours. It felt like days.

"Get up everyone!" my dad shouted. I sat up and rubbed my eyes. "Why are you looking so tired Dana?" he asked. "If only you knew" I said while laughing out of exhaustment. He gave me a weird look and then walked to the kitchen. I slowly got out of bed. "Are you okay sweetie? You look a little...Tired" Caleb's mom said. "I'm fine, it's just been a long night" I answered. She put her hand on my shoulder and smiled, before walking to the kitchen. I was dead inside, I really needed sleep. There's no way I would be able to train today. I went in the kitchen as the last person, so when I finally came, everyone were staring at me. I smiled awkwardly and took some cereal. We were all eating in silence. Like a dead silence. "The juice is really good" Owen's mom said, trying to make conversation, and after a while, pretty much everyone were talking about the juice while laughing. I didn't say anything. "What about you Dana, do you like the juice?" my dad asked while smiling. "Seriously? We're in a zombie apocalypse, and you're talking about some cheap juice from Walmart?" I blurted out in frustration. Now, the silence became even more silent, and all eyes were on me. "Okay" I chuckled in frustration. I put the dishes in the sink, and went to get some privacy. I looked around in the bunker. I found some boxes, and decided to find out, what was in them. It was mostly old toys and useless papers. But in the last box, there was a notebook. I slowly opened it. I started reading it.

I know I'm not crazy! Everybody thinks I am, but I know it's going to happen! There is going to be a zombie apocalypse! I know there is! And by the time it's gonna happen, I'm going to be too many steps ahead, for them to keep up! I'm gonna be prepared, and they will beg for forgiveness. I have a plan to solve it, but I'm gonna need some help, from people that actually believes me! And that's gonna be hard, but I will not let it pass me.....Never -James Stanley 12-03-2016

I couldn't believe it. If this person knows how to solve this whole thing, I'm gonna need to find him. I think we can help him. I kept on searching in the box for more information, but there was nothing. A lot of the pages in the notebook were apparently ripped out, so that letter is all the information I could get help from. So now, I just needed to find out, if hc's alive, and where he is.

-END OF 4TH CHAPTER-

-Chapter 5-

-James Stanley-

 I folded the note, and put it in my pocket. Should I tell the others about it? The answer is: probably. I would most likely not be able to hide, going in and out of the bunker, if that would become necessary.

I searched the entire bunker for more information about James, since I assumed he once lived here. I found an old radio with his name on it, but it wasn't working. Maybe I could fix it, and if I'm lucky enough, maybe he'll answer from another place. I used hours on trying to fix it, and the weird thing is, that it should be working now. Maybe it is working, but no one is just answering? I will keep trying, until someone responds...I have nothing better to do anyway. It was nice with a distraction from....Well everything. I was so tired. My eyes kept shutting, but I stayed awake. It was like that for a couple of minutes. My eyes felt like heavy rocks. The moment I finally left reality, and fell asleep, the radio turned on. The cracking radio sound made my eyes wide open. Finally, after 5 exhausting hours, it was finally working. This was my one chance, and I was not going to blow it, on drifting away to sleep. "Hello?" I said. Someone was trying to communicate with me, but it wasn't going through. "Please..." I said, holding my hands to my head. But after 7 seconds of plain cracking sounds, coming from the radio, it lost signal and shut off. "Damn it!" I shouted before kicking the radio in anger. "What's going on?" I heard a voice asking behind me. *No, no, no, no! Of ALL people, HIM!?* I slowly turned around, to see Owen looking down at me. "It's none of your business...." I mumbled in frustration. "So...You're still mad?" he asked while leaning against the wall. "Look, I've had a pretty shitty day...Or days. And the absolute last thing I need right now, is you pretending to be 'The good guy'" I said. "I'm sorry, okay! I just-". I cut him off. "Just what? Huh? You know what, just leave me alone dude". "Come on Dana!" he shouted after me. I was mad. Pissed. Frustrated. I

wanted to punch a wall. Scream. But there was
no way, that I was gonna break down. Not now.
I still have hope. Not much, but not nothing
either. I may have overreacted, but I think it was
just the whole zombie thing, that was making it
worse.

I stopped talking for a while. I needed time, plus,
it's hard getting privacy in a small bunker. It felt
like I was going crazy. I couldn't even get fresh
air, go for a walk, a run. I was starting to lose
hope...For myself. I just couldn't picture a
normal life, not anymore. Even if we did find a
cure, how am I supposed to forget it. Forget...All
the dead people. The people we couldn't save.
The people I watched transform in pain. I don't
think I can forget it...Ever.

The radio situation hit me bad. I stopped trying
for a while, which isn't...Me. After a couple of
days, I was ready to try again. I held the radio in
my hands in fear...In fear, that it would happen
all over again. That I had just wasted more time,
that I could've used on attempting to save people.

"Please work…" I whispered to myself. I turned it on and said: "James, if you can hear me, I'm gonna need you to answer me. Please. The world counts on you….". As more seconds passed without an answer, I lost all hope. *How could I seriously be so stupid?* I stood up, and started to walk away in disappointment. "Hello!? I'm here!" I heard a voice say. It came from the radio. I ran to the radio and kneeled down next to it. "James?…".

"Yeah?". "Oh my god…James, my name is Dana. I found your note, from uhm…2016, and uh…I think we can help you" I said. "Who's we?" he asked. "Me, my family and my friends". "What's your location?" he asked. "You know, the bunker I assumed you once lived in". "Yeah uh, right". We talked for a while. He lived alone, and would come to find me and the others. He said it was gonna take about 4 days. He sounded young, around my age. Now, the only thing I needed to do, was telling the others. It's harder than it seems. I haven't spoken in days, and I've been acting really distant and mad, so it was obviously awkward. I was trying to explain everything, but

I stumbled over my words. *Come on Dana. Just speak.* Finally. The words finally came out of me. I showed them the note too. "So?" I said. "Well, I think it's great!" my dad said. The others nodded. I sighed in relievement. *Thank god.* I trained the next couple of days, just in case James would say, that we had to go on some kind of a mission. I got stronger and stronger. Physically and mentally. It was nice with some space.

I didn't speak to Owen or Caleb. It just felt...Meaningless? I trained a lot. Not because I liked it *that* much, I just needed a distraction, and something to make the time go. I guess I've been needing a distraction more than I thought.

4 days passed. Today's the day James is coming. I was excited to see what he was planning. He sounded nice when we were talking. I couldn't sleep. I knew that I wasn't going to either, so I put my hair up, and started training. There was this creepy, old stunt doll, made out of wood, the same size as me, that I would use to train with. I

was kicking it. Punching it. As I did that, I felt my anger, slowly rising. I started kicking and punching faster, faster, and faster. It felt so amazing, but yet so pathetic. My movements were going faster, and I couldn't stop. The stunt doll was really hard. I couldn't control it. I started hearing a voice. It was too weak for me to understand. It got more and more clear, until I heard the word "Dana" being repeated. After a couple of seconds of confusion, I felt someone grabbing my arm. "Dana, you're bleeding". I looked at him. *You're bleeding.* Those were the words that kept repeating themselves in my head. As I slowly started to understand them, I looked down at my fists. He was right. I was bleeding. Warm, red blood, was dripping on the floor, coming from my fists. "Shit", I said quietly to myself. "What the hell were you doing?" he asked. "Training" I answered. "Are you okay?". "I think so" I chuckled, because I realized what had just happened. He pulled me into a hug. God it was embarrassing. I've never felt so pathetic. I buried my head in his chest, hugging him back. I didn't care about my madness in that moment. I slowly pulled away, to see my blood on his T-shirt. "Shit. I'm sorry" I said. "Don't be" he said. He squeezed my hand before walking back to bed. I sat down on the floor, while taking a deep breath. I laughed to myself. *You're so stupid.* I walked to the kitchen and got some paper, to stop the bleeding. I was exhausted.

As I heard banging on the door, coming from the outside, my eyes flew open. I looked around for a second. I guess I fell asleep on the counter. *Oh gosh.* I stood up, and looked through the little hole in the door. It was a boy. Around my age. It was James. I opened the door for him. "Hi" he said. I smiled and greeted him back. "Are you okay? No zombie attacks?" I asked. "I'm totally fine, thanks for asking". He smiled. I introduced myself and the others. We all sat down. Now, it was time to hear his plan.

-END OF 5TH CHAPTER-

-Chapter 6-

-The Venom plant-

"So James, what's your plan?" Caleb's dad asked. James opened his bag, and pulled out a homemade poster. He folded it out on the table. He pointed at a picture of a plant. "That's the Venom plant" he said. We all looked at each other in confusion. "And what exactly is that?" I asked. "The Venom plant was known for being super deadly if you came in any type of contact with it. It was one of the most suffering ways to die. Therefore, it was removed. If a Venom plant was spotted, it would be burned to ashes. After 2 years, there were no Venom plants left...or so we thought. It turns out, an unknown science man had found a Venom plant, and started growing his own. He experimented with them for a while. No one knew about it, until 2016 march 2nd. They tried to keep it a secret, so it wouldn't get too much attention, because they didn't wanted people to freak out" he said.

"Well why would they be freaking out?" I asked.

"Because...in one of the experiments, there was a
zombie created. It was killed quickly, but it was a
huge break through. The unknown science man
created another zombie, but kept it in a cage. He
ran other experiments on it, to find its
weaknesses and strengths. It turns out, the only
cure...is the Venom plant" he said.
"That doesn't make any sense. Why would it die
from the thing it was created by?" I asked.
"Because it wasn't created by the Venom plant.
It was created in an accident, that contained
human blood, chemicals, a dead body AND the
Venom plant. The Venom plant was the only way
to control the zombie. No one knows how, or
why Venom plants kills zombies, but it does.
Which is why-". "The cure is the Venom plant" I
interrupted. "Exactly. But the problem is, the
Venom plant is the most difficult thing to find.
But if we find out where the unknown science
man's lab is, we may be able to turn it into a gas,
that can be turned into some kind of a bomb, that
will kill all zombies" he said.
"But if it's so deadly...It will kill all humans too"
I said. "That's the problem. But if we can find

the part of the plant that kills zombies, maybe we're lucky enough that that part, is harmless to people. And it doesn't necessarily mean it has to be a miracle..." he said. "We're listening" I said. "Zombies are the opposite of humans, and the Venom plant contains 2 different types of gasses, that are the opposite of each other, and if I could get to experiment with a Venom plant, I would be able to find out, if one of the gasses are deadly to humans but not zombies, and if the other gas-".

"Is deadly to zombies but not humans, since humans and zombies are the opposite of each other, and so are the 2 different gasses of the Venom plant!" I interrupted again.

"Wow, you're almost doing my work for me" he said while laughing. I looked over at Owen who almost looked...Jealous? Or at least he didn't seem so happy. But why would he be jealous?

"I just have one Question" I said. James looked at me. "How did the zombie apocalypse happen?" I asked. "On October 14th, some experiment went wrong, and it caused a small explosion at the lab, which caused the zombie to escape. And since zombies are as aggressive as they are, they attacked many people really quickly, which made these people transform into zombies. Which caused the apocalypse to spread really fast, and that's also why you didn't find out about it on the news, since they didn't even had the time to make an episode or an announcement paper, before you found out" James explained. I started thinking.

"But...if we can find out, where the explosion happened, which shouldn't be that hard, we would find out where the lab is, since that's where it happened, right?" I said.

"Exactly! But by the time I was gonna find out where the lab is, you contacted me through the radio, and that meant I didn't have time to figure it out " James said. "Wait a minute...The lab exploded, which means everything in it did too" I said. "Not exactly. I read somewhere, that there's a basement, which is where the Venom plants could be at. And luckily for us, it's secured, so the lab did explode, but not the basement" James explained. I laughed a little bit in realievement. After a couple seconds I realized something.

"Wait...would it be possible to find an actual cure, that could transform the zombies into humans again, instead of the gas that is gonna get them all killed?" I asked.

"Hopefully...my aunt got transformed and uh...she's all I have left. I really don't want to lose her...for good" James replied.

"I'm sorry...But if it's possible, everybody will come back" I said.

"Not everyone. Zombies eat humans, so some people are completely dead, and can't be bringed back. The reason why people transform, are if they're bitten, but still survived the attack. The wound, or wounds, will get infected. Then fever, then personality and behavior changes, and then it infects the brain. We gotta stick together to make this plan work. You know, teamwork. We can actually end this..." he said. "Well...then let's start the research" I said.

-END OF 6TH CHAPTER-

-Chapter 7-

-The location-

I stood up and walked away. I heard someone behind me, and felt a hand on my shoulder.
"Hey, where are you going?" Owen asked.
"To find something we can do our research on" I answered while walking away again.
"Slow down" Owen said while catching up on me. "What?" I asked. "I just wondered...Are we good?". "Sure" I answered. "That's not really convincing" he said. "Well what do you want me to do about that?" I asked. "Mean it".

He was standing still, looking at me with a little bit of hope in his eyes. I couldn't believe him. He always does this. He says something he knows is gonna make me upset, and when I don't answer him, it makes me look like "The bad guy". I was in a too good mood to let him ruin it, as usual. I rolled my eyes and walked away. It felt toxic.
"Oh come on!" I heard Owen say from distance, but I kept on walking in frustration. I really

don't get why our relationship, always has to be so chaotic.

I remembered the time I found James note. The memory itself isn't so clear, but I do remember a bunch of "useless" newspapers, at the time, but in this case, they could possibly help us.

I went to the back of the bunker, where all the boxes with the newspapers in them are. I searched through every single box. It was just boring science stuff. I read every single word, on every single paper and...Nothing. Until the last newspaper I was reading. A word caught my eye. The word *lab*. The newspaper was from 2016, which was a pretty long time ago, but the location on the lab, was written on that page. "Yes!" I cheered.

The newspaper said:

AN UNKNOWN SCIENTIST HAS BEEN GROWING HIS OWN VENOM PLANTS FOR YEARS. THE LAB HE HAS BEEN CREATING THEM IN, IS IN OUR VERY OWN NOVALY, AT CONAENN STREET-

*My home town...it makes sense. That's why Novaly is hit bad...because that's where the explosion happened...*I stood up and walked to James. "Look..." I said before handing him the newspaper.
"You said you lived in Novaly, right?" he asked. I nodded. "Well do you remember anything happening when the lab exploded?" he asked. "It's a big town, and Conaenn street is *really* far away from where I live, so no, not really. Well now we got our location. How are we gonna get there?" I said. "I have a van, the one I came in" he answered. "That's perfect! When are we leaving then?" I asked. "Tomorrow?". "Sounds good" I said.
We talked for a while, just about our lives...nothing too crazy. It was getting pretty late. We needed to save energy if we're gonna have to fight against zombies. You always gotta be prepared.

I sat down on my hard matress and sighed. I was nervous, what if we can't find a cure? I was freaking out. I looked up and saw Dylan, Caleb and Owen enter the room. It felt weird not talking to Caleb. We're both people that moves on pretty quickly. They became silent when they saw me. I looked at them for a couple of seconds, before laying down and pulling the blankets over my shoulders. My bed was placed in the corner, luckily. So I turned my back on them to avoid eye contact. Everytime I shut my eyes, they opened again. I felt Owen's eyes on me. I didn't move...I was barely breathing. After a while, I finally fell asleep.

I felt someone's touch on my shoulders. Someone was shaking me. I was a little annoyed, and I'm usually not like that, but I finally had a good sleep, for the first time in a long time. No nightmares, no waking up in the middle of the night, just sleep. But we had an important mission, and I was more than ready for it.

-END OF 7TH CHAPTER-

-CHAPTER 8-

-THE GOODBYES-

I walked to the kitchen. Owen, Caleb, James and Dylan were there, and so was the adults. Owen sat on the middle chair, Dylan sat on the chair next to the wall, and Caleb sat on the chair closest to me. All the adults and James, had taken up all the other spots, so no matter where I sat, I was gonna sit next to Owen. I rolled my eyes knowing, that they planned it. That's probably why they were all together last night, when they walked in the big bedroom.

Both chairs were already pulled out for me. I sat down next to Dylan and Owen.
"Hey" Owen whispered to me. I didn't answer. The last thing I needed was more drama, and I was not gonna embarrass myself, in front of everyone at another breakfast. "I'm really sorry" Owen whispered. "You should be" I whispered back while smiling. He took my hand under the table. I would rather forgive him, than to be mad.

He didn't let go of my hand. He didn't wanted to. Not this time. I felt pretty good about forgiving him. It felt relieving. The big weighton my shoulders, was long gone. I took a deep breath.

We all ate. The food tasted better than usual. My laughs were finally made out of actual joy. I let myself think, that everything would stay the same. Just for a moment.

After a while, we were done talking, and we needed to get ready. I remembered a box of old jewelry, I found a while ago. I searched after it for a pretty long time, before finally finding it. There was bracelets, rings, necklaces's and earrings. But there was only 1 thing in the box, that got my attention. It was a beautiful, green bracelet, with a snake charm. I was amazed by how it affected me, because I couldn't get my eyes of it. I put it on, and then I went back to the others. Caleb's mom had already packed the food we were gonna bring.

"Here you go" she said before handing the backpack to Caleb. Me and Caleb made eye contact. It was weird between us. It had been such a long time since our fight, but we still hadn't talked. I turned around before it would get awkward, and made my way towards James. "Are you ready?" I asked him. He nodded. "Alright, let's find the lab" I said. It was only me, Owen, James and Caleb that were gonna go. But we had the radio with us, and walkie talkies...Just in case.

I looked around and saw Dylan in the corner. He didn't exactly look happy. I slowly walked towards him. He sat in an old chair, that were covered in spider web. He avoided my eyes. I could see he was hurt. I looked at him for awhile, not knowing what to say. "I don't want you to leave" he confessed, still looking down. I sighed. "I'm gonna be okay. We all are. If we don't do this, no one else will, and we gotta be fast, before too many people transform...In case we can't find a cure, that won't completely kill them" I said while putting my hand on his shoulder. He faced me. I smiled slightly. He nodded while taking a deep breath. I pulled him into a long hug. I didn't wanted to let go, but I knew everyone were waiting for me, because I felt eyes on me. "Okay..." I whispered while pulling away. I walked towards James. I made my finale goodbyes, and then we walked up the stairs, and out of the bunker. As Caleb opened the big door, I had my gun ready...But there were no zombies. We ran to the van, and now...I was ready to find the cure, to end this hell.

-END OF 8TH CHAPTER-

-CHAPTER 9-

-THE TRIP-

When we were all in the van, Owen closed the door, and James started the car. He started driving, and there was a deadly silence. Everything about it felt wrong. I felt like I was breathing too loud, swallowing too loud, and it was really awkward. I wished for the car ride to go faster, than I knew it was going to be. The hours felt long. Sometimes James would start to hum. Everytime he did, I tried to listen closely, to figure out what song it was. After some time, I finally figured out, that he was humming "We are young".

As he started humming again, I joined. "And you feel like falling down, I'll carry you home, tonight. We are young" I sang. "So let's set the world on fire, we can burn brighter than the sun...Tonight, we are young" Owen interrupted. We all started laughing. It wasn't as awkward anymore. I looked to my right, to see Owen staring at me. As my look rested in his eyes, I started feeling better. More safe. One of the windows wasn't closed all the way, so the wind had found a way in. It was playing with my hair and on my shoulders. It held the smell of flowers. It kinda reminded me of spring, even though it's fall. "How long do you think the mission will take?" I asked James. "It depends on what we find".

As the time flew by, the smell of flowers faded away, but a new smell appeared. I couldn't figure out what exactly it was, but what it definitely was not, was enjoyable. The others started to smell it too. "Oh god, what is that?" Caleb asked. We all started coughing. I started to recognize the buildings. We were in Novaly...Our city...Also the city with the most zombies. The city was almost...Unrecognizable. That's why it smelled so awful. More zombies appeared, which also meant, that more zombies were chasing the van. "Shit" I mumbled, looking through the window. The others saw it too. James started to speed up, and after 7 minutes, we lost them.

"Thank god" Owen said. My hand rested on my chest in relievement. And just as I thought the zombies were gone, something bumped into the van. There was something on the window. It almost looked like...Blood. But it was blue. A human figure stood up, right in front of the window. But it was not a human. Actually the opposite. James froze. He was staring at the zombie in disbelief. "DRIVE!" I shouted. He quickly came back to reality, and pressed his food against the speeder. As he was driving away, I looked back, and the zombie was completely smashed, and lifeless. My breathing was heavy, as I was in shock.

We had been driving for 6 hours, and it was slowly starting to get dark. I reached under the seat, and grabbed the blankets. I gave one to Owen, and to Caleb. I laid down on my back, and stared up at the ceiling. I pulled the blanket over my neck, while I was shaking, because of how cold it was. I started humming. I was humming the song, my mom used to sing for me, right before bedtime. "As deeper as it goes, as scarier it gets, but if you don't fall, you never get hurt. So when..." I sang quietly. I tried to open my mouth, to continue. But every time I tried to, the song was gone. I had to realize, that the song was fading away from my memory. But the worst part about it was, that I also had to realize, that I was slowly forgetting my mom's voice. I tried to think of every memory I have of her, but her voice was gone. My worst nightmare.

I turned around, so I was facing the wall. My heart felt empty. This was the absolute worst thing that could possibly happen. I used to hear my mom sing in the kitchen every single morning, and now, I couldn't even remember her voice. As a warm tear was rolling down my face, I closed my eyes. I fell asleep pretty fast. I was so exhausted.

I woke up to a loud noise. It was James. "We're here!" he said. I rubbed my eyes and stood up. I looked out of the window. He was right. We had arrived to the lab. It was surrounded by signs. It was being cleaned. I realized that the green bracelet with the snake charm wasn't around my wrist. "Oh no. Shit" I said, trying to look for it. "What's wrong?" James asked. "I lost my bracelet. It's green, and has a snake charm" I said. "We'll look for it later" James said. We all had our guns ready, as we stepped out of the van. But there were no zombies. We walked towards what once was a lab. I kicked one of the signs to the ground. "Are you guys ready?" James asked. "More ready than ever" Caleb said.

-END OF 9TH CHAPTER-

-Chapter 10-

-The lab-

We walked towards the lem, that would bring us to the lab. There was dust everywhere. I got to go first. I slowly opened the lem, and crawled down the ladder. There was a long way down. I finally reached the ground, after a couple of minutes. It smelled so awful. I turned around. It was huge, and there were plants and chemicals everywhere. The boys were now here as well. They looked around. "Wow..." Caleb said, with wide open eyes. James looked around fascinated. He touched all the stuff as he was looking around.

Something caught my eye. It looked like blood...But the blue-ish blood, that came from the zombie. "Hhm" I said under my breath. James came closer. "Is that...?". "I think so" I answered. He took the container with the zombie blood, and put it in a plastic bag, and then in a bigger bag. "It could be useful" he said. "How?" I asked. "Maybe if we can't find the Venom plant,

we can use the blood instead, to see if there's
Venom plant in that blood". I nodded slowly.

We looked everywhere. Every corner, every
paper, every chemical, every plant, every dusty
drawer...But nothing. The Venom plant wasn't
anywhere in the lab. We were reading every
word, on every paper, with a hope, that maybe
we would find something. I rolled my eyes, after
reading lots of pages, of no helpful information. I
picked up another paper, and started reading. It
was a printed link. I tried searching after the link
on the laptop we found, and it brought me to
some messages. The messages were about The
old farm shop, which is near my house. My uncle
works there as well...Well, he used to. "Oh my
god..." I whispered under my breath. It turned
out, that that's where the Venom plants are. I
had come there so many times, but I never knew.
Had my uncle ever even been aware?

James looked in my direction. "What?" he asked.
I stared at the dusty laptop screen. "I guess
we're at the wrong place" I said. "What do you

mean?" he asked. He stood up and walked towards me and the laptop. He started reading the messages. I looked at him. His face expression was...Well, he looked happy and annoyed at the same time. It was understandable. I mean, of course he's happy that we now know where the Venom plant is growing, but annoyed that we are at the wrong place, and that The old farm shop isn't secured for zombies, so it's a big risk. And you know, the longer it takes to find the cure, the more people have transformed, so if we can't find a cure that won't not kill them, then that means...You know. "Let's go" James said. "What, why?" Owen asked. As James were preparing the tour out of the lab, I explained it to Owen and Caleb. They didn't know how to feel about it either.

James had his gun ready, and he started crawling up the ladder. We were right after him. He opened the lem carefully, and crawled out. We were all up. There weren't any zombies. We all ran to the van. As Caleb was getting in, something appeared behind him. You've probably already guessed what. He stopped to look back. I pulled him in by his arm quickly, right before James pulled out his gun. I covered Caleb's eyes with my hands, and pulled him into my chest. I flinched as the gun went off.

I slowly opened my eyes. I looked at Owen. He was staring at something behind me. He looked at me. It looked like he felt sorry for me or something. He was for sure in shock. "What?" I asked. There was silence. He took his eyes off me, and looked behind me again. I was confused, but I followed his look, and turned around. He was looking at the zombie. It was on the ground, not fully dead. I was still confused. But after a couple of seconds, it made sense.

My heart sank. I couldn't breathe or move. *No.* I didn't know what to do. I wanted to scream, but nothing could come out. I let go of Caleb. He looked at my wet eyes. He was confused, until he turned around. I slowly walked towards the zombie. My legs were too weak to hold me up any longer, so I fell down on my knees, beside the zombie. I stared at it in disbelief. I stared at *her* in disbelief. "Mom...?". I had so many questions. I thought I was gonna throw up. "Mom!" I cried. She looked at me. She knew it was me. She tried to say something, but she was too weak. She hadn't fully transformed yet. She took my hand. "Where have you been!? I thought you were dead! I thought...". A tear was rolling down her cheek. "Dana?" she managed to say. How could she even remember, if she's a zombie? Everything was blurry. I heard weak footsteps behind me. Someone pulled me away. "NO! MOM!" I screamed. I tried to fight, whoever was pulling me into the van. I saw Caleb closing the door. I was banging on the door crying, while my mom was looking at me. I was crying. Harder than ever. James started the car. "No!" I cried out of breath. I looked up, and saw another zombie running towards the van. That's why they pulled me away. I looked down at my mom. She was shot in the leg, so maybe she could survive. They drove away, right before the zombie got to us. I was crying, while snot was running out of my nose, and I had the worst

headache ever. I started to recognize the touch.
It was Owen holding me. He was the one who
saved me. He risked his life for me.

He held me close. I couldn't breathe. After 7
years, I finally saw her. I didn't think she was
alive. I was mad. *Really* mad. I turned around.
Shit. So many things were going through my
brain, but yet, I couldn't think. I jumped at
James. I was out of control. He didn't even know
it was her. It wasn't his fault. But I let my rage
take over. I tightened my grip around his throat.
I was *actually* trying to strangle him. Owen
pulled me away. James was gasping for air.
Caleb took over wheel, before we crashed. I was
realizing what I had just done. "Oh my
god...I'm...I didn't..." I said. James was in shock.
I couldn't blame him. I mean, I just tried to kill
him. My stomach felt weird. Kinda empty. It felt
like there was no air in my chest. She was alive.
She never died. But I'm probably never going to
know what happened. I might never hear her
voice, or her laugh again. I couldn't get the

image, of her looking at me, out of my head. I felt guilty. My mom. My innocent mom.

-END OF 10TH CHAPTER-

-Chapter 11-

-The old farm shop-

I sat in the corner. Caleb and Owen were asleep.
James and me, were the only ones awake.
"I'm really sorry" I said. He kept quiet. He was
mad. I don't blame him. I wouldn't forgive me, if
I was him either. I sighed, and then laid down.
"What happened to her?" James asked. I slightly
panicked since I didn't know what to say.
"Uh...She went missing...7 years ago". He didn't
say anything. Minutes passed by, and I knew he
wasn't going to say more, so I turned around and
closed my eyes. I couldn't sleep. At all. My face
felt hot. A tear rolled down my cheek. And then
another one...And another. I couldn't forget the
fact, that I met my mom...And that I'll probably
never know what actually happened to
her...Where she was for 7 years...What she was
doing. 7 years in pain...All for nothing.

I didn't sleep that night. I threw up twice. We
stopped after 3 hours, so that James could get

some rest. Now, I was the only one awake. The whole day just replayed itself in my head. Over and over.

It was 7 AM. I started seeing black dots in the corners of my vision. *Oh no.* I tried standing up, because I couldn't think clear. The dots became bigger. I put my head in between my legs, for blood to come to my head. The dots disappeared, but I couldn't breathe. I thought I was overreacting. *Shit.* I knew I wasn't supposed to do it, but I needed air. I opened the door and collapsed on the ground. I was struggling to breathe, but it slowly became easier and easier. I was finally okay.

I heard something behind me. "What are you doing?" I heard someone ask. I turned around. It was James. He must've heard me. I was just staring at him. I tried to speak, but nothing would come out. He reached for my arm. After I had a good grip around his wrist, he pulled me up.

"Thank you". We quickly went back in the car, and James closed the door. "Now, tell me what happened" he said. "I think I was fainting". He nodded and sat down in his seat. I went in the back of the van, and laid down. James started driving. I was a bit surprised, that I didn't wake neither Caleb or Owen.

After 28 minutes, we arrived to The old farm shop. I woke up Owen and Caleb, while James made sure that there weren't any zombies. I was kinda surprised, when he came back saying, that there weren't any, but then I remembered, that it makes the chances for the Venom plant to be there, bigger, since zombies avoid Venom plants. We went inside, with our guns ready, of course. We looked around and started investigating. The shop was completely ruined. It made me a bit sad to see it like that. I've come here since I was a kid.

Everything were covered in either dust or spiderweb. Something smelled really bad, but I had gotten used to it. I started to look in some of the drawers. There were som cash, candy and lots of papers. As my eyes were running over the

pages, I was looking for the word *Venom*. I
didn't find anything, but then I noticed, that
there was a drawer with a lock on it. It was
hidden. I looked around for something to break
up the lock.
Come on. I remembered something. I went to the
back room, and found the toolbox.
When I went back to the drawer, I was holding a
hammer. I hit the lock one time. Nothing. Then a
second time. Almost there. On my third try, I got
the lock open. I quickly opened the drawer.
More papers? I started reading yet again. Only 3
papers in, I found something. *Bingo.* "James, you
might wanna take a look at this". James gently
took the paper, and started reading. He looked at
me. "This is it" he whispered. I smiled, of the
thought of coming back to the others.
I walked towards the 'Employes only' door, that
I had never been aloud to go in. The floor was
made of wood. There was a secret door
somewhere in the floor. Me and James started
searching. It didn't take long before we found it.
I crawled down the small ladder, and couldn't
believe my eyes. *Oh my god.* "Yes!" I shouted.

This room...Was filled with Venom plants. God it smelled awful, but the sight was amazing considering, that we were tired, and wanted everything to be over. James was happy as well. I could see the joy in his eyes. The last sparkle of hope. He took some pictures with a small camera. I was about to touch one. "Be careful!" James said. "Don't forget that the Venom plant is deadly". Thank god I didn't touch it. Caleb and Owen came. "Holy shit" Caleb laughed. James started to do his weird nerd stuff, and then put some plants in special bags. I looked over at Owen. He didn't pay any attention to me staring, he just admired the plants. I noticed, that the walls had weird holes in them. Everybody seemed busy. *Oh well.* I crawled up the ladder, and started investigating more in the shop. *Ew.* The shop was gross. And how? It had only been a few weeks. Or...Maybe not. I don't...Remember. I've completely lost track of time. I heard noises. I turned around. The boys were coming up. "We need to find a lab. The nearest one" James said. I started thinking. "I have a plan" I said. **-END OF 11TH CHAPTER-**

-CHAPTER 12-

-BACK AGAIN-

It was 2 hours later. We were on a bumpy road. I was taking a nap, surprisingly. "And we have arrived!" I heard James cheering. I opened my eyes. We were back. I was back. It felt strange. We stepped out of the car. I was holding a gun in my left hand . We slowly headed towards the door, and Caleb opened it. *Oh. My. God.* It looked awful. Worse than awful. "Think about how much missed homework we must have" Owen said. "Yeah. I have not missed school" I said.

"Let's head up to the chemistry lab".

"You guide me" James laughed.

We got to the staircase. *Holy shit.* There was blood everywhere. Blue and red. "I don't wanna go through that" Owen said. "Too bad" I responded, before walking upstairs. I tried to avoid the blood, but some did get on my shoes. The boys were right behind me. We got to the chemistry lab, but it was locked. We all tried to

kick it, but it wasn't working. "We'll split up and try to find something. We'll meet here in 10 minutes, with whatever we've found" James commanded. James and Owen walked away, so me and Caleb were stuck together on this little mission. We started walking in the opposite direction of the others. I completely lost focus as we walked past the classroom I was in, when the siren went off. "Come on Dana" Caleb said. I snapped back and followed Caleb. We walked in the janitors room, and found a hammer. "Why would the janitor have a hammer?". "No clue". We brought it with us, and started walking back. "Did you hear that?" Caleb asked. "What?". I was confused...But not for long. One of the doors flew open, and it was filled with hungry zombies. "Shit!" I yelled. We started shooting on them. "How could we have missed them?!" Caleb shouted. There were too many zombies, and I was running out of armor. I pulled Caleb by his wrist and we started running. "What do we do!?" he shouted. "The roof!".
We started running up towards the roof. "Close it!". Caleb closed the door, but it couldn't lock.

"Shit! What do we do!?" I asked. We hid behind a metal thing, and as I heard the door open, I sealed Caleb's mouth with my hand. We had trapped ourselves up here. Basically commited suicide. I was shaking. He was shaking. We were definitely doomed. "I have a plan" I whispered. "On three, we run back in the school again, and close the door after us. And then we just run". Caleb nodded. "On three. One. Two...Three!". We ran and closed the door, just in time before the zombies had acknowledged we were there. Luckily, we could lock it from the inside. "Run!" I shouted. It didn't take long before we heard, that the zombies had kicked the door open. "Holy shit! They're stronger than I thought!" I said. This was bad. *Really* bad. I started hearing someone yelling in distance. It must have been Owen and James. We followed the sounds, and saw them from a distance. I ran faster when I saw Owen. I jumped in his arms. "Oh thank god you're alive!" he said. I was relieved as well. "Do you have armor?" I asked them. They both nodded. "We gotta kill these motherfu-" I said before James covered my mouth. The zombies

had catched up. Me and Caleb stood behind
James and Owen, and they started shooting.
There weren't many left. "We're out of armor!"
James shouted. *Oh shit.* There were 5 zombies
left. I remembered I had a knife in my back
pocket. I pulled it out and held it in my hand.
"Die, you piece of shit!". I threw my knife at one
of the zombies. It landed in its chest, and the
zombie fell down on its knees, lifeless. I gasped
in shock, since I expected to miss. One of the
guys pulled me by my wrist, and we all started
running. James suddenly took a turn, but the
rest of us didn't have time to run back after him.
"What the hell is he doing?!" Owen asked in
frustration. We were all running out of breath,
but we hid in a classroom just in time before
we'd probably have collapsed. I could feel my
heart racing. Unnaturally fast. I couldn't even
focus on a thought. It felt like I was
hyperventilating. "What do we do if they come in
here?" Caleb asked in a whisper voice. Owen
shrugged his shoulders. There were no windows
or vents in here. "We gotta find James" Caleb

said. "Now!?" Owen argued. "You've got a better time!?".

I heard something. "Shut up!" I said. They both became quiet. *James.* I stood up and ran out of the classroom. I saw James in the end of the hall. "James?". I ran towards him. He was holding something...He was holding...I got close enough to see what was in his hand. He was holding the Venom plant. He was wearing thick gloves. I smiled. "Remember not to touch it" James laughed. I looked to my left, and there were 4 dead zombies. "How did you-". "Don't ask" he said. That's why he took that turn. He had to go back to where he had placed his bags with the plants and gloves. Owen and Caleb appeared behind me. They realized what had happen as they saw the Venom plant.

"Here's the plan. We find more armor, and then secure the entire school for zombies. Together this time" James said. I nodded.

About an hour later, we were finally done.We found about 11 more zombies in total, but they were dead now. In the room the zombies had broken out of, back when they chased me and

Caleb, we found human parts, which is why they hadn't broken out of the room before, since they were eating. We used everything we had found earlier, to break down the door to the chemistry lab. James had brought a dead zombie in there, to study it. Couldn't be me. He started on all his nerdy stuff, and we weren't aloud to touch anything. It was a bit boring.
"Wait...Do you guys remember the lake near by?" Owen asked. "Oh my god, we could go for swims and finally get clean!" I said in excitement. We all agreed that it was a good idea. We just needed to bring weapons, and we'd probably be fine. "We will probably need clean clothes" Caleb said. We decided to break the lockers open, to see if we could find clothes. It may have been weird and gross, but we were desperate. We all ended up finding clothes we could wear after the baths. We took every piece of clothes we found, and put everything in bags, so that when we returned to the bunker, the others could get clean clothes as well. We found towels in the PE locker rooms, that we were going to use for the baths too. It might have been

stealing, but at this point, who was there to care? James paused his nerdy stuff, and we all headed down to the lake. We had our guns ready, if anything were to happen. The lake was only 2 minutes away, so it didn't take long before we were there. We did see a couple of zombies, but we kept quiet, so they didn't see us. It was going to be a quick swim, but anything would help at this point.

"Do you guys remember when everyone would sneak down here at summer after school?" Caleb asked. "Of course we remember" Owen answered. We went one by one, and the others waiting would close their eyes while turning the other way. It was my turn. I stepped into the water carefully. It was extremely cold, since it's fall. Or wait...Is it winter? I had no idea. I counted to 3, and then went under water with my head. It was awful, but yet very refreshing. I felt 10 times more awake. I brushed through my hair with my fingers, and made sure to wash my armpits extra. I finally got out of the cold water. I was freezing. A lot. I had goosebumps. I dried myself with the towel, before wrapping myself

in. When we had all washed ourselves, we washed our dirty clothes in the water as well. We quickly went back into the school. It was way warmer in here than before. I went into the ladies bathroom, and put on some of the clothes I had found earlier. It was thick jeans and a brown sweater. As I was walking out of the bathroom, I remembered something. I ran upstairs and into the classroom I was in when the siren had went off. *There!* I spotted my backpack, and I opened it. *Bingo.* It felt so good to hold it again. My beloved phone. The first thing I checked was the date, of course. It said...November 19th. *Wow...Already?* If the explosion happened October 14th, then it had been 37 days. I put my phone in my back pocket and walked downstairs to the others. I looked around. They were gone. I looked in the other halls. Nothing.
Where could they have gone? I started walking towards the big doors, that would lead me into the gym. They were sitting in a circle. "What are you doing?" I asked confused. James held up a radio. *Ohh!* We had completely forgotten to contact our families at the bunker. The walkie

talkies we had brought, obviously wouldn't work, because of the distance, but the radio might. I decided to show them my phone. "Where did you get that?" Owen asked. "In my backpack I had left here. Is the radio working?". "Almost" James answered concentrated. It was saying weird, cracky noises. Just like the time I tried to contact James. "For how long have you been trying to reach them?" I asked. "A couple minutes" Owen responded.

Some time passed by, but nothing seemed to happen. We eventually gave up, and decided it was time to get some rest.

-END OF 12TH CHAPTER-

-Chapter 13-

-The reunion-

We split up to go find some blankets and pillows. I went with James, but we decided to go up to the roof instead, just for some time. It was chilly outside, but I didn't really mind. I laid down and looked at the stars. I heard James laying down next to me. "Have you lost any friends? You know, after this whole...Zombie thing" James asked. *That's...Random.* "Uh...Not really. It's just me, Owen and Caleb". "Oh" James said surprised. "I've just never really been good at making friends...So" I said, out of awkwardness. "Yeah, I get that. Everyone thought I was crazy, since I would always talk about how I knew the zombie apocalypse was going to happen. After that, no one really wanted to be friends with me" he said. "Oh...I'm so sorry. That must've felt lonely".

James sighed and turned his head to look at me. My eyes met with his.

"Well now I have you guys" he said. I smiled a little out of sympathy. "We should probably get back" I said. James nodded and we headed back to the gym. Owen and Caleb were already there, and they had brought some blankets and pillows. "You didn't find anything?" Owen asked. I shook my head, trying to hide my smile. Before we went to bed, we put locks on the doors, so that the zombies hopefully couldn't break in, or at least not without us hearing it.

We all laid down under our blankets. "So, what do we do tomorrow?" Caleb asked. "Tomorrow we head back to the bunker, to get your families, and then we will go to my house, since I have a lab there, and all my resources. And there...We will create the gass bomb" James said. "Is it a bomb? It sounds so...Dramatic" Caleb asked. "Well not exactly. It's a little hard to explain, but let's just say it contains the gas, that will transform the zombies back into humans".
"Wait, so you found a way that the gas won't kill zombies? But just...Transform them back?" I asked in excitement. James nodded with a smile. "After hours of investigation, yes, I did".

"Seriously?!" Owen cheered. We were all happy, but most of all relieved.

I laid back down and closed my eyes. I fell asleep surprisingly fast. I had a dream that night. Not a nightmare, but a dream. It was beautiful. I was laying on a field. It was late summer, but warm. Not sweating warm, but like a nice warm. Even though there was a breeze, it still wasn't cold. It was night. There were stars everywhere, and it was a clear sky, no clouds or anything. I was all alone, but I didn't feel lonely. It was peaceful. The silence was peaceful. I didn't have any thoughts about a stressful future, or a chaotic past. There was thunder, but I wasn't scared, even though I was laying on a flat field, with no trees, or taller objects than me. I felt safe, and then I woke up. The light made my eyes shut immediately. I let out a disappointed sigh. If only I could've stayed in the dream. Somebody started pulling my arm. "Come on Dana, we gotta pack everything, and get going" Owen said. I rubbed my eyes and blinked a few times, to get use to the light. I stood up and made my way towards

the bathroom, before I had to help pack. I looked
at myself in the mirror. I had an idea.
I smashed the mirror, and picked up the big
pieces. I accidentally cut myself. *Damn it*. I went
into one of the stalls to get paper. I wrapped it
around my hand. I went back to the gym with
the mirror pieces, and put them in one of the
bags we had found. "We're all ready" James
said. "So we have the medical kits from the
office?" I asked.
"Check" James responded. "Blankets and
pillows?". "Check". "Tools from the janitors
room?". "Check". "And clothes from Lost and
found?". "Check". "Well then we're all good" I
said with a smile. We all put at least 1 bag over
each shoulder, and then went to the front of the
school, and unlocked the doors. "Are you guys
ready?" Owen asked. We all nodded in silence.
Owen opened the doors, and we rushed to the
van. Caleb closed the car door, and James rushed
to the wheel, put the keys in, and stepped on the
gas. "I never thought I would get to sleep in the
school" I laughed. "Me neither" Owen chuckled.
"That's for sure a sleepover I'll never forget" I

said, while looking out of the window. I looked back to see a few zombies running after the car. I informed James about it, but he didn't speed up.

"I gotta save the gas. There isn't much left" James said. "Is it possible we could make a quick pit stop, to fill up the car, and maybe get some food?" Caleb asked. "My thoughts exactly, but we've got to lose the zombies first" James responded. We arrived at a gas station soon after, and while James got the gas, I went inside, to get food. There weren't much left, but I took everything I could. I went back and put it in the van, and I waited outside, to enjoy the fresh air, as long as I could. As I was looking at the sky, I noticed a group of birds. They were flying away from Novaly, the same direction we were going. *That's weird.* I noticed something in a distance. I let out a gasp. Caleb noticed me, and looked the same way I was looking. A big group of zombies were coming...Towards *us*. They weren't that far away. "James hurry!" I shouted.

"Why?" he asked, right before noticing the zombies. "Shit" he said quietly. We all rushed to the van, but the zombies had catched up. James stepped on the gas, and we drove away quickly. I wave of relief hit me, until a hard knock nearly smashed the window. A zombie was on the roof. "Shake it off!" Owen yelled to James. "The van isn't in that kind of condition!" James yelled back. Caleb took a gun, and rolled down the window. "Caleb!" Owen shouted. Caleb struggled to shoot it, as he couldn't see it. A gun shot went off. Then another one. And then one more. Finally the zombie rolled off of the car, and fell on the road. Dead. "Are you okay?" I asked. He had his back turned and didn't respond. I slightly tapped him on the shoulder. He turned to look at me, but when I saw his arm, I froze in disbelief. *No.* "You're...bitten" I whispered to myself. Caleb stared at the wound. "I'm gonna die" he said. He kept repeating himself. "You're gonna be fine!" I shouted, because he wasn't listening. "Uh...I mean, the wound isn't big, so by the time you would transform, we would hopefully have released the gas" James explained. *How could this happen?* I took out the medical kit, and put on gloves, before I cleaned the wound. "Get some rest everyone" James said. We all took out our blankets and tried to sleep. I had a weird feeling in my stomach. I was scared. *Really* scared. Owen and James were asleep. I kept on hearing Caleb turning. I assume he couldn't get comfortable in a position. "Caleb" I said. "Yeah?". "Relax. You're gonna be fine. We're gonna help you. Cure you, and protect you. And we won't leave you" I said to calm him down. He didn't answer. He must have been freaking out. I drifted off to sleep eventually.I had a nightmare about Caleb transforming. I woke up. It was only James who was awake. I looked at my phone. It was 9:11 AM. My battery was low. I could probably get a charger at James' house. "How many hours until we're back?" I asked James. "About 2" he replied. I was tired, and went back to sleep.

"Dana, wake up. We're back". I opened my eyes. I looked around, and noticed the bunker outside. "Come on, hurry" Owen said. I took my blanket and pillow, and we rushed to the bunker, and knocked on the door as hard as we could. When I

saw my dad's face, I felt a wave of happiness.
We quickly went inside. As soon as the door was
shut and locked, I melted into my dad's arms. He
held me close. I froze. How was I going to tell
him about mom? He pulled away and looked at
me. "We were worried! Why didn't you contact
us!?" he asked. "We were just really busy
and...We kinda forgot to. But we actually tried
once, with the radio, but you didn't respond" I
replied. Suddenly Dylan came, and hugged me.
Really tight. "Okay, okay I can't breathe" I
laughed. Caleb's parents were hugging him.
Owen was in his mothers arms. I hadn't missed
the bunker, but luckily, we weren't staying for
long.

-END OF 13TH CHAPTER-

-Chapter 14-
-The gas-

We packed all the useful things in the bunker, which was how the rest of the day went by. We also gave the rest of our families the clothes we took at the school, and they were very excited. Caleb's parents hadn't reacted very good to his wound…When the darkness took over, we all went to sleep. The next morning we were prepared and ready to go. It was going to be a long trip. 4 days. That's how long it took for James to find us. "Everyone ready?" Owen's mom asked. We all agreed it was time. Everybody rushed to the van. It was really crowded. I had just started getting used to only being 4 people in it. James and my dad had made a plan, about the driving situation. James would drive at day time, since he knows where we are going, and then my dad would drive at night, and would get a map.

It had been 7 hours since we started driving. "Is your house zombie secured" I asked James. He nodded. Everything was so boring. I just wanted to teleport to the destination. "Can we have a pit stop?" Dylan asked. "Yeah, sure" James responded. He stopped near by the woods. I waited till everyone was out, until I stepped out of the van. I stretched my legs, and went somewhere in the forest to pee. When I was done, I came back to the van, and waited for everyone. James came next to me and leaned against the van. "So, are you excited to come back to your own home?" I asked him. "Yes, I've missed my own bed" he laughed. Caleb came over. "Hey, we should probably clean your wound" I informed him. He nodded, and we went inside the van. I opened the medical kit, and started cleaning his wound. It was awkward, and I was out of conversations. I finished and put all the medicine back, and then I covered the wound with a plaster. "We're gonna put a new plaster on, and clean the wound every single day" I said. He didn't respond, but I didn't know how to comfort him. Everybody eventually came to the van, and we were ready to go. James started driving. After another 2 hours, it was getting

dark. My dad took over the wheel, and everybody else tried to get some sleep. I fell asleep after about 10 minutes of constantly turning, trying to find a comfortable position. When I woke up, James was driving again. Owen's mom and Caleb's parents were awake. "What time is it?" I said rubbing my eyes. "About 09:15 AM" James responded. I slept well. My stomach felt empty and started growling. I ate some of the snacks we had stolen from the gas station. After an hour had went by, everyone had eventually woken up. Hours kept on passing by, and every single one, felt like a whole day. I felt the space crawling up on me, slowly. Trapping me. The lungs becoming hard to fill up with air, and the desperation of freedom growing, spreading and eating me from the inside out. Most of the time in the van, I would close my eyes, and imagine my life in the past. Before all of this. When everything was normal. Decent. Bearable.
I'd imagine myself getting ready school. I use to hate it. Getting ready knowing, that I was going to have a bad day, but coming home telling my

dad it had been fine. Fine. F-i-n-e. What I now would do for my life to be 'fine'...

2 days later we had finally arrived. James house was literally in the middle of nowhere. Far out on the farm. It was quite peaceful. There was a fence around the garden. "Are those spikes on top of the fence?" I asked James. He nodded before going outside to open the gate. He came back and drove the van in on the property, and then closed the gate. It was a nice little house he had. It almost looked like mine, if it was blue and had more windows. "God I've missed it" I heard James say under his breath. He walked towards the entrance, but kneeled down in front of a plant. He lifted up the potted plant, and took the key that was hidden beneath it. *Sneaky.* We just have ours hidden underneath the doormat. He opened the door and we all entered inside. It was cozy and nice. There were many plants and candles. I looked around, until I saw a picture on the wall. It was a woman with James. I assume it's his aunt. A bittersweet feeling appeared in

me. I walked away and spotted James outside. He was trying to open a door to a shed, but it was locked with a chain. I went outside to figure out what he was doing. He looked frustrated. "What's the matter?" I asked him. "I forgot where I put the key" he said, holding his face in his hands. "We could just smash the lock" I suggested. "Yeah" he nodded. He told me to follow him, and we ended up behind the house. There was a pile of rocks. "What the hell" I said. "I tried to collect as many forms of weapons I could, when the apocalypse started, 'kay?" he said while lifting up the biggest rock there was in the pile. We went back to the shed, and he tried to smash the lock. 6 tries later, the lock was smashed and the chain had fallen off. I kicked in the door, and was amazed by what I saw on the inside.

"This is *my* very own lab, that I spent most of my time in. All of my tries and experiments were made in this exact shed" he said proudly, while I looked around, trying my best not to touch anything. "This is where we will be creating the gas in the container" he said.

"Alright, I'll be back in a few" I said before walking back into the house.

-END OF 14TH CHAPTER-

-CHAPTER 15-

-THE TRANSFORMATION-

I looked around for some time, until I found him. "Caleb?" I asked. He looked up in shock. "Oh sorry, I didn't mean to scare you" I laughed. "Well I think it's time to clean your wound" I said. I went to get the medical kit, and when I came back, Caleb looked really upset. "Why are you crying?" I asked, kneeling down next to him. "I don't wanna die" he whispered. God, those words hurt me, right in the chest. "You won't. We've got this under control. I promise. We won't leave you" I comforted him. "What if I hurt you?" he asked. "Then...We'll handle that too, somehow". I pulled his sleeve up, and ripped off the plaster. *Oh my god.* His wound...Was getting worse. It looked infected. Badly. "Still think it's gonna be fine?" Caleb scoffed in anger. I hesitated. "Yes" I responded.
"Oh come on! I can see it all over your face, you liar!" he raised his voice. "Okay, fine! It's bad, and you probably won't make it to christmas, but we will lock you up, and won't leave you. Is that

what you wanted to hear?" I asked in frustration. He already knew, before I even told him, but he still looked shocked...Because it was true, and he was finally facing it. If we hadn't cleaned his wound every day, he would probably be transforming already. I started cleaning his wound twice a day, instead of just one, and change his plaster twice as well...But it still didn't help with the infection. It only postponed his transformation. Along with that, James was really fighting for that cure. He worked hard, and made a lot of progress all the time.

It was December 13th. The last week had been hard for Caleb. He had started having cravings for food. He ate. All the time, but nothing stopped his hunger. It wasn't a good sign. I noticed slight changes in his behaving and personality. He was moody, angry and a bit aggressive sometimes. Those were signs of his transformation, since zombies are found to act aggressive. I woke up, and it was Friday. I went downstairs to get some breakfast. I thought I was the only one awake, until I heard something...From the kitchen. I turned around the corner and saw Caleb. He was eating something, but I couldn't see what it was. He was on the floor, with his back turned to me. I got closer, and my eyes widened. There was blood. I let out a gasp, but I got an even bigger shock, when his head turned and he looked at me. It only took me a moment to see, that that wasn't the Caleb I know. His eyes...Were shiny. They had a wrong glance to them, and behind the two dark brown eyes, there was nothing, but an infected brain. No soul. No Caleb. My eyes moved further down, and I saw his...Meal. A squirrel. I didn't waste a second, and I began to run...But he was chasing after me. I screamed, to try and wake everyone up. I quickly got into the bathroom and shut the door. But he was fast, and he had put his hand trough the door opening before I had closed it. Now it was me against him. We were both pushing, and it was only up to our strength.

A cold fear ran down my spine, because I knew I didn't stand a chance. Especially not against his zombie strength. I was about to lose when all of a sudden, the door closed with no power against it. I won? There was no way. I couldn't hear him anymore, it was completely silent. I held my breath, until I heard James. "Dana? Are you okay!?" he asked, knocking on the door. I opened up, and saw Caleb on the ground, and James in front of him, holding a bat. "Oh thank god" I whined in relieve, before hugging James. "Did he get you?". "No, no. I'm totally fine". Owen came storming. "Oh my god" he whispered. "What did you do!?" Owen yelled at James. "I saved your girlfriend for you, that's what I did. I'd appreciate a 'Thank you' next time, smart ass" he hissed back. Owen looked offended. He walked over to me and hugged me. "Are you okay? Tell me what happened" he asked me. "I'm fine. I came down and saw Caleb eating a squirrel, and then he saw me and...He...He chased after me. I tried closing the door to the bathroom, and he was trying to open it, and then James luckily came and knocked him out before he got to me" I explained. "We've gotta lock him up in a safe container, out in my lab" James said. We all agreed, and we carried Caleb out in the lab, and locked him up. "He can't get out. Trust me" James assured us. Caleb slowly woke up. He started to aggressively pound on the glass, while screaming. "When will he stop?" I asked. "Zombies don't need sleep, so he probably won't" James responded. I left the lab and went inside. When I entered, everyone was looking around. "There you are! What happened?" my dad asked, while everyone were waiting confused for my answer. I tried to talk, but I couldn't. I didn't know what to say, or how to say it, so I just broke down. My dad was holding me on the ground, trying to understand what had happened. "It's Caleb..." I managed to say. Caleb's parents looked at me in shock, and they started crying. Owen came inside, and broke down as well. His mom was hugging him as tight as she could, trying to calm him down.

A while later, dad was trying to comfort me, in me and Dylan's room. I was laying on the bed, with dad sitting down next to me, and Dylan was in the chair. "I need to tell you something..." I said. "Oh no, you're making me worried" dad said. "When I was on that trip with the others...I found something...Someone" I confessed. "Alright, who?" he asked. "I saw...mom". His eyes widened, and he teared up. "We were getting into the van, and a zombie appeared behind Caleb. James shot it, but then I saw that...It was her. It was mom. I went over to her, and she did recognize me, even though she was transformed. But I got pulled away and..." I couldn't finish that sentence, as I was overloaded with guilt, for leaving her. He looked confused, but yet understanding. Dylan started crying. *Shit.* I forgot he was there. He ran out, crying. Well, he had to get the news somehow. Dad wiped off his tears and went to get Dylan. I broke down. Why was all of this happening? And why was it happening to me? It was all for nothing. Absolutely nothing.

-END OF 15TH CHAPTER-

CHAPTER 16

-NEW YEARS EVENING-

Days passed by, and Dylan had a hard time dealing with the news about mom. So had dad. James had been working. Day and night. And it was time. We had been putting up traps to capture rats, squirrels and mouses, so that Caleb could get some food. He was always pounding on the glass, trying to get out, but the container was solid, and he couldn't break it. Owen had been helping me a lot. Mentally.

It was December 26th, and the gas was ready to be released. We were going to release it in Novaly, at the airport. It would take 5 days to get there. We would arrive at New Years evening, if everything went as planned. We weren't all going to go. Only me, Owen, James and dad. The others had to stay back and watch Caleb and Dylan. Plus, all the parents are not as athletic and flexible as us, the teens. My dad is coming so that he and James can switch with driving, and so that we can get the extra power. For example if we were to carry something heavy. Plus he is smarter than us. Well, maybe not James, I'll let that stay a mystery. We had packed everything. We attached a trailer to the van, where the container will be placed in. I said my goodbyes to Dylan, and then we made our way to the van. I was not excited for the trip. At all. I had just gotten used to living in an actual house. I was really starting to have love-hate relationship with the van. It's great and big, but yet so little and disgusting. The plan was that James would drive half of the trip, all the way to around the old bunker, and then dad would drive the other half, since he only knew the way to Novaly from the bunker. James had brought his laptop, and I decided I would try and watch something, if I had Wifi. "What's the password?" I asked James. "IloveCassie112" he responded. "Who's Cassie?" I laughed. "My aunt. She made the password when I got the laptop for my 16th birthday" he answered. I typed it in, and it worked.

"Let's try to go on Netflix" I said to myself. I clicked on the logo, and waited with crossed fingers. It was loading for a good amount of time. "Come on" Owen whined, with his fingers crossed as well. The Netflix intro appeared on the screen, and we all started cheering. "Oh thank god" I laughed. "What shall we watch?" Owen asked jokily. "I never got to watch season 3 of '22 minds'!" I said in realization. "Shit, me neither" Owen laughed. The season had just gotten out, right before the apocalypse. It was one of my favorite shows. It was about a lab experiment that had gone wrong, and 22 of the people that had gotten experimented on escaped during a fire alarm. They all had powers, that they only managed to control, because of the medicine they had gotten in the lab. But since they were on their own, long gone, they couldn't control their powers on their own. It's amazing. I got to meet Number 021, who's one of the three main characters. She's so pretty. I started the first episode of season 3. "Can you turn it up" James asked, even though he was driving. I turned it up, and that's what we did on day 1. Day 2, we watched 3 movies: Katerina, Forever hers and Hidden in the shadows. Day 3 we were pretty tired, and I slept through almost half of the day. But we just watched "Rotten". A popular series that I never wanted to watch, but it turned out to be kind of good. Day 4 we finished the series, and discovered online Uno. We played that the rest of the day. December 31st, day 5, we were getting ready for the final day of this hell. It was going to end, today. 10 AM, and we had arrived at the airport, but we had a group of zombies that had followed us here. Me and Owen started shooting at them, as soon as we stepped out of the van. After 11 shots, around 9 dead zombies were on the ground. "Shit" I groaned. "I think we got them all" Owen said. Well think again. The gunshots had attracted a group of at least 30 zombies. Maybe we should start considering, that guns probably weren't the smartest weapons to use. "Oh lord" I whispered. "Get in the car!" dad screamed. We rushed in the car, and dad started driving around on the field, with the zombies chasing after us. "What do we do!?" James shouted. "Dad roll down the windows!" I screamed. He did what I told him to, and I shouted: "Shoot them god dammit!" to the boys.

We all started shooting. *Shit.* I reloaded. Around 10 zombies were left, but they were very close to the van. We're talking only 10 meters. "Speed up!" Owen shouted to my dad. "The van can't go faster than this!" dad shouted back. "Garbage...Throw garbage at them!" James screamed. "Jesus!" I shouted as I rushed to find garbage. We had a couple garbage bags, full with all the trash we had collected over the month. We started throwing them out the windows, aiming after the 10 zombies. It slowed them down. The second one James threw, landed right at one of the zombies, and it fell right onto its back. "Now! Start shooting" I shouted. We all tried to shoot them, but it was quite hard as the van was driving at the same time. After many gunshots, it was over. "Jesus" James groaned. I sat down and rested my head against the wall, and sighed of relief. I opened my eyes and saw a group of birds, flying away from the airport. "No time to waste" dad said before opening the door. We all left the van, and started setting up the container. It took a while, because god it's huge. It started getting dark. "It's ready" James said.

Me and Owen made our way inside the airport, with weapons of course, and walked around for a bit. We found the snack shop. It was almost empty, but there were still lots of food left. We started eating some chocolate bars, and I found some gummy worms. "I'm so ready for this to be over" I laughed. Owen agreed. I looked out of the window to see if everything was okay. They still hadn't released the gas. A movement further away caught my attention. Nothing was there...Or so I thought. A group of around 40 zombies were making their way towards James and dad. I took out my walkie talkie. "James?" I said. "What's up?" he responded. "There are zombies coming your way" I said. I saw him turn around. He took out his gun, but I didn't hear any gunshots. "Shit! I have no amour left!" he said over the walkie talkie. "We're coming! Try and get to the van!" I said. Me and Owen ran outside and got our guns ready. "We don't have enough to kill them all" Owen said. "Uh Dana?!" James said over the walkie. "We don't have the goddamn keys!" James panted as they were running away. My heart skipped a beat, and I realized *I* had the keys. Dad had asked me to hold them as they were setting up the container, but I had forgotten to give them back. "I have them! But there's no way we can make it to you guys in time, before the zombies have catched up on you!" I said. Some seconds filled with silence passed since we didn't know what to do. "Why the hell did you guys run in the goddamn opposite direction of us?!" I asked as tears were filling my eyes. "We didn't think about that!" James yelled over the walkie. The zombies had almost gotten to them. Owen suddenly screamed. Very loud. The zombies turned around, and started running after us. "What the fuck!" I yelled at Owen. We were running back to the airport, with the zombies right after us. We finally got inside. Owen held my face, and I saw he had watery eyes. "You go hide and I'll distract them. When you know they've passed you, you run. You run as fast as you can back to the others with the keys! I'll try and shoot as many as possible, and get them as far away from here as I can!" he said. "But...You won't..." I said as my voice was breaking. "No 'buts'...I love

you" he said as a tear rolled down his cheek. He
ran away while yelling as loudly as he could. It
was too late for me to follow him. I rushed to go
hide behind a sign. I got there just in time before
the zombies had stormed inside, following
Owen's yells. I was covering my mouth, trying
not to make any sound. The zombies had passed
by and was far enough away, for it to be safe
enough for me to run outside. I ran. Faster than
I ever had. I was crying. When I finally made it
to James and dad, I dropped to my knees of
exhaustment, and cried out loud. I couldn't
breathe. I couldn't see anything, because my
tears were covering my sight. I tried to talk but I
didn't know what to say, or how to say it.
Eventually I got out the keys and we rushed to
the van. When the door was closed and locked,
dad came to me. "Where's Owen?" he asked in a
serious tone. I opened my mouth, but nothing
would come out. I covered my face with my
hands and cried even more. "No...no, no, no" I
was whispering to myself in denial of what had
just happened. There was no way, that he could
possibly survive. I finally explained to them what

Owen had done. They were shocked, and neither knew what to say. "You have to go release the gas NOW! He's buying you guys time" I said. They rushed outside while I stayed in the van. I felt sick to my stomach. Why was all of this happening to me? And what did I do to deserve it? What did any of us do to deserve it? Had I really been *that* bad for all of this to happen to me? First mom, then Caleb and now Owen. I was hoping and praying that Caleb could be brung back. How was I ever going to move on with life if this "gas thing" worked? How could I possibly ever be happy again? I started to lose all faith and hope. Not for this situation, but for me. I stood up and grabbed my gun. I looked down at it. Considering. But my mind was overflooded with all my memories with dad and Dylan. I couldn't do it. Not to them. They didn't deserve that. I put the gun back into my pocket. The door suddenly opened, and my heart skipped 2 beats. It was just James and dad. "It's done" dad said. I let out a laugh. James and dad hugged me. We were all relieved. We stayed in the car over night, with turns on watches. I took most of them, as I couldn't sleep anyways. Not after what happened...In the morning we decided to go out and look around, to see if it had worked. We walked into the airport, and had our guns ready. A wave of overwhelming happiness washed over me, when I saw a big group of people, gathered together. James put his hands to his head in shock. "It worked...It worked!" I yelled. We started cheering. After going through literal hell, the apocalypse was over. The group of people were all confused. We explained what had happened, and they were shocked. They didn't seem to remember. They were all very pale, and covered in blood. They stunk. *Very* badly. After that, it was time to go back to the others.

-THE END OF 16TH CHAPTER-

After 5 days we were back to James' house. 2023 had been the worst year of my entire life, but it was finally over. The gas had not gotten all the way over here. I was heartbroken when I had to tell Owen's mom about...You know. She completely lost it. 3 days later we found her in the bathroom. She had taken a shit load of pills and didn't make it. I can't imagine losing your husband and then your kid. She had nothing left, since she had not had any contact to her parents for 7 years. We started to get help and made a plan with some people. James was going to produce more gas, and then they were going to release it around the US. After we had some more gas, we released it inside Caleb's container. He transformed back, and we let him out. I hugged him for a long time. He looked in a bad condition. He looked like a ghost. His vision had gotten worse, and he had headaches all the time. We got some medical help for him. After he had gotten more normal and was functioning like a human, we told him about everything. He couldn't remember. I had to tell him about Owen. He was devasted. He must have been so overwhelmed. I was by his side most of the time.

I'd usually try and avoid mirrors. I hated what I saw. I hated myself. I was so pathetic. I had literally tried to strangle James to death, I had acted like such a self-absorbed coward towards Owen, when he was alive, and I had let him die. I had left my own mom. I had killed people. So many people. Even though they were zombies, they were somehow still people. I had acted so cold towards everyone that I've ever cared about. I hated myself. I despised myself. "Myself". I don't even know who I am anymore. I only felt two things towards myself; Hate and disgust.

It was March 14th. I was at home, emailing interviewers back. It felt like a normal day to me. Or at least as normal as it could get. There was a knock at the front door. I heard dad getting it, so I just stayed in my room. When I finished with my emails, I closed my laptop, and made my way downstairs, to see who was at the door. I walked down the stairs, and took a turn around the corner. Dad was hugging someone. It sounded like he was...Crying? "Dad?" I said. He pulled away from the person he was hugging, and turned to me. He stepped aside, and I could finally see the person he had hugged. I froze. I couldn't move or say anything. "Oh my god" she said. "Mom?". "Hi" she chuckled before running to me. She was holding me tight. Even just her scent was comforting. She had survived the shot in her leg, and had been transformed back by the gas. She slowly pulled away, so she could look me in the eyes. She wiped away my tears. She looked normal. Way better than last time I saw her. I was struck by joy, it was overwhelming. "What happened to you?" I asked just before my voice broke. "I was kidnapped" she confessed. "Are- Are you okay?" I asked worried with tears streaming down my face. "I am now, yes" she laughed, and pulled me into her arms again.

Nothing really went back to normal. There were a lot of "missing" posters around. I had nightmares about Owen, every single night, but mom was always there, comforting me. School first opened up again 6 months later. Hospitals were overfilled with people. All the previous zombies. Almost ¼ of the US population were gone. Dead. Missing. That's a lot of people. The apocalypse didn't spread any further than USA, luckily. James had found his aunt. Our story was extremely popular. "The Novaly kids who saved the world". Almost everyone knew who me, James and Caleb were. We were practically famous. We had an interview today. July 8th 2024. I was nervous. Dylan had helped me get ready, well, he picked out my outfit. I met up with Caleb and James in front of the building where we were going to film the interview. We all went inside and got greeted with cheers and applause. I hated it. I didn't like the way I had so many eyes on me all the time. I've always been used to being kind of invisible. I liked it that way. I wasn't very comfortable during the interview. I hoped it wasn't visible. We told our story, from each of our perspectives. I spoke about Owen, but I didn't wanted to share too much. "Dana, did you know there's a hashtag for Owen that is currently trending?" the interviewer asked me. "Oh...Uh no, I did not" I laughed. "Oh there is! It's #OwenIsOurHero" she said. I nodded and smiled, trying to cover up my anger. None of them even knew him, and he got treated like shit by literally everyone at school. People are so fake. The interview continued. "Do you have any knowledge about the virus?" we got asked. James talked about the venom plant and how the apocalypse started. They were about to move on, but I stepped in. "I noticed that birds could sense the zombies. Right before big groups of zombies would come to us, I usually noticed birds flying in the opposite direction. And there were barely any birds in Novaly". Someone behind the camera was taking notes. I became nervous. What if I had said something wrong, but just hadn't noticed? After we had been there for an hour, it was finally over. I felt sick. I rushed to the bathroom. As I looked in the mirror, I had a flashback. I was very pale, just like the day the apocalypse started. I had never had a flashback. Not like this one. It was weird and quite overwhelming. It felt like the air was getting so thick, that I couldn't breathe it. My heart was racing so fast, it felt like...Dying. I thought I was going to die. I was sliding down the wall, and as I reached the floor, I brought my legs to me chest, and hugged myself, as the only source of comfort I could get at that moment. Someone knocked on the door. I couldn't really say anything, as I was already struggling to breathe. The door flew open, and dad rushed to me. He was trying to comfort me. He was slowly helping me to breathe. After some time, I finally got it under control. I was confused, and just wanted to go home. "You just experienced a panick attack, Dana. Do you know what that is?" he said. I nodded. I had never felt this way. I mean I had heard a lot about panick attacks and anxiety, but I never thought it would happen to me.

It was getting dark and dad was driving me home. I looked out of the window. I was thinking about my future. What was it gonna look like? I had no idea. Was I ever going to find love? Was I ever going to find happiness? Could I ever possibly move on from Owen? Would everything ever go back to normal? It probably couldn't. At least not for me.

-END OF 17TH CHAPTER-

-CHAPTER 18-

-HAPPINESS-

I felt movements on the bed. I groaned as I opened my eyes. "Mom, Dad! Wake up!". "It's christmas!". I smiled. "Go check if Santa have been here" I said to them. Melody and Florence jumped down from the bed and ran out of the room, all the way downstairs. I rubbed my eyes and turned my head. He was already looking at me. "We better go down there before they rip open all of the presents" he said. I laughed. We both left the bed, I put on some slippers, put my hair up in a ponytail, and then we went downstairs. Melody was jumping around and Florence was attempting to feel the presents, but she got caught right hand. "Oohh someone's busted!" I said before chasing after her. She's not that fast so I got her pretty quickly and started tickling her. She was laughing and screaming. "No mercy!" I said in a low tone. I stopped and turned around to look at him. He nodded. "Present time!" I cheered. They were both squealing and jumping in excitement. They opened up their presents. When there was only air under the tree, I went out to the kitchen and grabbed it. I came back and told them to sit. They did and I revealed the present I had hidden behind my back. Melody could barely keep it together. "You guys can open it. Together" I said. They did and each pulled out their bracelets.

"These two bracelets are very special, so you'll have to be very careful with them, which I thought you guys are finally old enough to do, since you both just turned 8. You're now big girls. I got the bracelet that you're holing Florence, when I turned 8. And the one you're holding Melody, was my mom's. They are 'best friends bracelets', and since you're so big now, I thought I'd pass them onto you guys" I explained. They got excited about them, and promised to protect them with their lives. After that, they started playing with their new presents, and there was a knock on the door. "Who's that?" he asked. "I don't know, I'll go check". I rushed to the door and looked through the little hole. *No way!* I quickly opened the door.

"Oh my god, James! Hi!" I laughed, and went in
for a hug. "Hi Dana" he chuckled. "What are
you doing here?" I asked. "I was coming here for
work and thought I'd stop by. And I uh...I
brought this for you" he said before handing me
a present. "Oh. I feel bad I don't have anything
to give you" I said looking at the present.
"Don't" he smiled. "Oh uh, come in!" I said. "Oh
no that's fine! I just wanted to come see you and
give you that" he said pointing to the gift. I
laughed and opened it. It was the green bracelet
with the snake charm, I had lost in the van. "Oh
my god. I had forgotten all about it. Thank you,
James" I said. "No problem. I was cleaning out
the van to sell it, and found it between two
seats". I smiled while adoring it. I put it on.
"Well I better get going. Merry christmas Dana"
he said. "Merry christmas" I chuckled before
closing the door. "Who was it?" Anthony smiled.
"Just...An old friend...Wait, what's the time?" I
asked. "10:26" he said. "Oh shit! I'm gonna be
late!". I quickly grabbed my keys and my bag,
and kissed him on the cheek. "Love you!" I yelled
while running outside to my car. I drove fast and

arrived 2 minutes late. I rushed to the door and knocked. Gabriella opened the door. "Hey Dana!"she said and gave me a hug. "Hi Gabbie" I greeted back. "Hellooo sunshine!" Caleb laughed. "Sorry I'm late" I said while taking off my shoes. "It's good, no worries" he said. I took off my jacket as well and made my way in the living room. I gasped. "Cookies!" I said. Caleb laughed, and we sat down at the table. "Sooo, how's it going with the twins and Anthony?" he asked. "Very good! Uh...So James showed up at my house today" I said. "No way!". "Yeah, he gave me this bracelet" I said and showed it to him. "The bracelet you lost in his van!" he said. "Yup. I haven't seen him in years, you know, since he became so busy with work and lived so far away" I said. "That's insane. What did he look like?" he asked. "Older...Oh and he had a beard!". "No way!". We catched up and ate some cookies. After 2 hours I had to get going. I said my goodbyes and drove to the next destination. I smiled in comfort. There's nothing better than your childhood home. I knocked at the door, and Dylan opened it for me. "Hi! You're here early" I said hugging him. I took off my shoes and jacket and went to the livingroom. That's where I found mom and dad. They were both sitting in the couch, listening to christmas music. "Hi guys!" I smiled. "Dana!" dad said hugging me. "Hi sweetie" mom greeted back and hugged me as well. Dylan came and joined us on the couch. We opened presents, chatted and sang together. It was getting dark and it was time for me to go home. As I drove home, it started snowing. When I entered inside I saw Anthony asleep on the couch with the twins. My heart melted, and a smile appeared on my face. Music was playing on the radio. I was overwhelmed with joy. I had found love, which I never thought was possible after Owen. I had started a family. That's when I finally realized. This was what I had searched for. What I had wondered if I ever would get to feel again. What I needed. What I had longed after. Happiness.

-THE END-

Leia F.L

I am very happy about finishing this book. It has been fun and quite difficult to write. It is my 3rd book in total, but my first English one. I am from Denmark, but I have family from USA, and they have not been able to read my other books, as they are written in Danish. I hope they enjoy this book, along with everybody else, because it was a true pleasure to write. And of course I had to give Dana her happy ending ;)

-Leia F.L

© 2022 Leia Falkenberg Larsen
Publisher: BoD – Books on Demand, Hellerup, Denmark
Print: BoD – Books on Demand, Norderstedt, Germany
ISBN: 9788743047810